# Someone N

Anne Sibley O'Brien

Charlesbridge

For Jean Keene, librarian and book lover, with deep appreciation for your love and support through the years

## Acknowledgments

I'm grateful to many folks who helped make this book happen.

Thanks for input, inspiration, and support to Sarah Sheridan's fifth graders at Kishwaukee Elementary School in Rockford, Illinois, and Karen Bieschke, Pam and Jim Keeling, and Sunil Puri of Rockford's annual International Day of Peace; and to my writing comrades, Liza Keierleber and Sarah Thomson.

Thanks for Photoshop technical assistance to Marty Braun, and to Taz Sibley for his heroic, last-minute rescue of my files.

And once again, for everything else, thanks to my editor Julie Bliven, art director Susan Sherman, and the whole crew at Charlesbridge.

First paperback edition 2021
Copyright © 2018 by Anne Sibley O'Brien
All rights reserved, including the right of reproduction in whole or in part in any form. Charlesbridge and colophon are registered trademarks of Charlesbridge Publishing, Inc.

At the time of publication, all URLs printed in this book were accurate and active. Charlesbridge and the author are not responsible for the content or accessibility of any website.

Published by Charlesbridge
9 Galen Street
Watertown, MA 02472
(617) 926-0329
www.charlesbridge.com

Illustrations done in watercolor on Arches 60-lb. watercolor paper and colored digitally
Display type set in Hunniwell by Aah Yes Fonts
Text type set in Tonic by Tomi Haaparanta
Color separations by Colourscan Print Co Pte Ltd, Singapore
Printed by C & C Offset Printing Co. Ltd. in Shenzhen, Guangdong, China
Production supervision by Brian G. Walker
Designed by Whitney Leader-Picone

Library of Congress Cataloging-in-Publication Data
Names: O'Brien, Anne Sibley, author, illustrator.
Title: Someone new / Anne Sibley O'Brien.
Description: Watertown, MA : Charlesbridge, [2018] | Summary: When three children, Jesse, Jason, and Emma, are confronted with new classmates from different ethnic backgrounds, they strive to overcome their initial reactions, and to understand, accept, and welcome Maria, Jin, and Fatima.
Identifiers: LCCN 2017028984 (print) | LCCN 2017041655 (ebook) | ISBN 9781632897152 (ebook) | ISBN 9781632897169 (ebook pdf) | ISBN 9781580898317 (reinforced for library use) | ISBN 9781623542696 (paperback)
Subjects: LCSH: Difference (Psychology)—Juvenile fiction. | Social acceptance—Juvenile fiction. | Ethnicity—Juvenile fiction. | Ethnic barriers—Juvenile fiction. | Conduct of life—Juvenile fiction. | CYAC: Difference (Psychology)—Fiction. | Conduct of life—Fiction. | Ethnicity—Fiction. | Friendship—Fiction.
Classification: LCC PZ7.O1267 (ebook) | LCC PZ7.O1267 So 2018 (print) | DDC 813.54 [E] –dc23
LC record available at https://lccn.loc.gov/2017028984

Printed in China
(hc) 10 9 8 7 6 5 4 3
(pb) 10 9 8 7 6 5 4 3 2 1

# There's someone new in my class.

# There's someone new in my class.

Jin just arrived. He loves to write stories.

# There's someone new in my class.

**The new girl** comes from another country.

She's trying to learn English.

She looks like she wants to speak.

But she doesn't say a word.

At recess, she just stands there, watching.

Does she want to play? Does she know how?

Our team is great as it is. I don't want to mess it up.

The new boy looks frustrated.

I remember what it was like when I first got here.

Everyone else was connected like pieces in a puzzle.

I was the different piece that didn't fit in.

I would share my comic, but he can't read or write.
I don't know how to figure out this puzzle.
I wish I had a superpower to help him.

The new girl seems strange to me.

Everything about her looks different.

It feels like there's a big distance between us.

I don't know how to reach her.

I try to explain what we're working on.
She doesn't understand anything I say.
I don't know how to make her feel at home.

Um . . . we're making pictures about our community.

I feel uncomfortable.

I don't know what to do.

I can't figure out how to help.

**One day** Maria comes up to me.

I guess she's been practicing speaking.

I can understand her.

She's so brave to ask to play.

I say we give Maria a chance.
A few kids on our team don't like that.
But maybe she can play.

Does she even know how to play?

What if she's no good?

Why do you want *her* on our team?

Let's see what she can do.

Game after game, Maria is unstoppable.
Turns out she played every day back home.
She didn't want to leave, but it wasn't safe for her parents.
She had to come here.

She may not know many words, but she can play.

We're even better with Maria.

On our team, there's room for more.

Jin has been practicing writing.

He shows me what he wrote.

I can't read it. It's like a secret code.

He shrugs. I shrug, too.

It feels silly, so I smile. Jin smiles back.

We both start to laugh.

Maybe a smile is like a superpower.

One day I help him with his letters.

We practice together.

Jin teaches me how to write in his first language.

It's like we have a real secret code!

This is your name in Korean. Jason. *Jae-sun.*

Wow, cool!

I bring in my favorite comic books to share.

We start to make up our own stories.

It's hard to remember a time when Jin wasn't here.

**Most** of the time Fatimah is gone to another class.

When she comes back for art, she just sits there.

She stares down at the blank paper.

She never looks up.

I make a picture of Fatimah and me.
When I give it to her, she looks at me.
There's light in her eyes.

The next day I draw my family and my house.

Fatimah draws her family and her house.

She adds flames and soldiers with guns.

She shows me how her family ran away to another country.

We draw more pictures together.

Fatimah's colors get brighter and brighter.

I have two brothers, too.

We learn more and more about each other.

Someone new is part of our team.

Someone new opens my eyes.

Someone new is my friend.

# A Note from the Author

In *Someone New*, Jesse, Jason, and Emma each meet a new classmate who seems different from them. Imagine encountering someone you've never met before, someone who, on the surface, doesn't seem to be like you or most people you know. You might wonder: *Will I be able to communicate? Do we have anything in common? What if I make a mistake?* It's possible you may have even heard things that make you nervous about a group the person belongs to. What will your friends say if you're seen with this new person? This type of discomfort is called *intergroup anxiety*. It can keep us from connecting across differences or changing our limited ideas about other people.

As Jesse, Jason, and Emma eventually discover, there are things we can do to reduce intergroup anxiety. I've had lots of experiences of this in my own life. Moving to South Korea from the United States as a young girl, I was often the new, different person. On the flip side, I've also been the one with the opportunity to welcome new people to my community. Again and again I've noticed that when I dare to reach out, that first response of discomfort shifts. A connection can be as simple as giving a smile, saying "Hi, my name is . . .", or sharing a seat, a meal, or a story. Bit by bit the barriers between us dissolve and the new person comes into focus. I'm often amazed to discover how much I have in common with someone who is so "different" from me.

We can overcome intergroup anxiety even by *imagining* a positive connection. When Jesse thinks that Maria might make a good member of the team, when Jason imagines himself as a superhero rescuing Jin, and when Emma makes a picture of herself and Fatimah together, each of them is actually creating the possibility of friendship with their new classmates.

*Someone New* was created as a companion to *I'm New Here*, which introduced newly-arrived students Maria, Jin, and Fatimah. This time around I chose to return to the same story and look at it from the point of view of the three students who were already "home." Each of them, for different reasons, has to move through discomfort in order to welcome the new student—and make a new friend.

Books are a wonderful way to learn about other people's lives and to imagine positive connections across differences. To continue to create community through sharing books, visit "I'm Your Neighbor"— a project that promotes literature featuring new arrivals and includes an extensive list of recommended titles at **www.imyourneighborbooks.org**. Further resources for exploring *I'm New Here* and *Someone New* are available at **www.annesibleyobrien.com**.